The Konpeitō

Masquerade

by

Big Sal

The Konpeitō

Masquerade

ISBN – 978-1-7347162-6-9

Covers: Wolf Proctor and Tamara Twa
Production: Jacob "Big Sal" Luna-Cantor
Copyediting: Jacob "Big Sal" Luna-Cantor
Research: Jacob "Big Sal" Luna-Cantor

Printed in the USA
KDP printing/2021

PART I –
"Home"

"To my oldest son, I love you and I'm sorry I'm not the best version of myself I can be for you. I will continue to try and succeed at being a good person and father until the day my breaths of fresh air turn into dirt or ash. May your path forever be walked alongside the righteous and the bodies of invading marauders. This one is for you, bubba. Love ya to the moon and back."

- Your Dad

Table of Contents

Introduction [Skit]

The airship cut through the atmosphere like a papal blade through tendons of an angel wing, and it wasn't long before the weather calmed enough to touch down just outside the grime-weeping city.

Sal and his son, San, stepped forth from the metallic rigidness of the stairs leading down to the radioactive dust and decay below as they took their first steps unto this fetid old world.

Father and Son, hand-in-hand, together they would reconquer the planet before it devoured them, and it was only through sheer willpower and dedicated observation did Sal manage to see his target nearby. "Look there boy, you see that pathway there in the distance? I think that's it. Come and follow me so we can check it out."

Taken together and amongst the ashes, the faded cobblestone path that Sal and San were walking on was soon overgrown and engulfed in a series of dark oak trees lined on each side of the beaten area like executioners awaiting a common goal.

In the fog of the war-torn wounds left upon the earth, Sal pointed towards the off-white mansion at the end of the road and nestled snugly behind a cover of more bramble, briar, and oak guardians.

Father and Son came upon the decaying remains of what was once a rich man's home as well as obviously the site of several conflict-ridden events that seemed to run down the ruins even further – like a sweet tooth with sugar!

Sal could feel the ominous energy present in the area and he prepared to leave back to the ship when he heard his son perk up behind him, "Hey, daddy, look I found an old book!".

Sal took his boy by the shoulder as they sat on a large stone and gently dusted off the leather-bound cover of the journal with the name, "Gaspar".

PART II –

"Arrival"

Trail of the Sweet Smoke

Grasses touch streets and skies when they're passing through here later,

Ashen dust eats the eyes on an avenue or acre,

Why take the truth a one-way if it burnt the books we're dumping?

I paid my dues on Sunday and I heard the wolves were coming,

Tie desire down the blaze while I stand down my death,

I was tired out of place and a man out of depth,

Amounts that pool our money goals and sought the dead awake,

The town was full of hungry souls and not of bread to break,

Throwing bodies down like Panem or a devil with the stainless,

So, they sought me out in tandem and the kettle that I came with,

Near the meadows and the millet cut for smiles to waste the weeds,

Here the devils in the village come for miles to taste the sweets,

Find the sun and fallen bridge at the cesspool that you fall in,

I'm the one they call a witch with my kettle and my cauldron,

Dead as autumn's winter tears as they cut a tree so rigid,

Yet their problem disappears when they come to me to fix it,

I might've paid to stash cash if fouler men were costly,

The night I made my last batch, a shadow entered softly,

Though he's man enough to run in with his sons to break and steal,

So, I'm standing at the oven as he comes to make a deal.

An Affront to Gods Everywhere

Try to cure me if it's looking like a hand that courted taste,

I was nearly finished cooking when the man aborted grace,

Candles seeping to the mortar as the engine broke a cog,

Shadows creeping in the corner and its mist could choke the fog,

It's sad to be a pot of gold if asked to be a common goal,

This shadowy simpatico just has to be as prodigal,

Pits nasty and impossible to pass with lots of dead to stack,

If ashy as a hotter coal when asked and offered heaven back,

Near the dam that frets the rain if it broke from pyrolysis,

Here the man he said his name as he spoke in hieroglyphics,

From the sand and gilded root as I dug up what I cradled,

In his hand he held a cube as it spun up like an angel,

It's water for a fireman when tossed by the breach,

The offer was retirement and walks by the beach,

Since the broken brought a number to a new plate of lonely,

In a moment saw my summer as it soon faded slowly,

Pierce this can of punch soda past the melted brick and lantern,

Here the man was hunched over as he held a fig and gandered,

Stand as hazy next to diction as it holds its weight in water,

An amazing recollection with an ultimatum offer.

9.

The Snap of a Dragon

The catacombs a dusty chance to do more than an oak,

The man that's known as Huxley sat in stupor as he spoke,

Restack the beans and come back when your stories are in color,

He had the dreams in one hand and the warnings in another,

Stand to jack the last havens in sagging flak that hath saved him,

Snapping back like snap dragons and adding crack to map flagons,

Cost them dough to work and show by a soldier's certain goal,

Watch them go berserk and blow like an old convertible,

Show a cop to a Christian, sowing thoughts like division,

Blow the top like an engine; no one stops for a prison,

Though the clock isn't tickin' – growing moss on a pigeon,

Woe the god in your vision knowing loss is prevention,

Stow the gun to haul money if to trod past a rose,

So, the one we call Huxley hits the shop as we close,

Freeze or fuse him to the putrid on the canvas of defeat,

He's perusing to the music like his hand is in the wheat,

It's a pal that waited months for the laughs in the cabbage,

With an elevated touch on the chaff in the rapids,

Kiss the guile of the same men that enact a holy hate,

With the smile of a dragon as he snapped to show me fate.

A Baker's Dirty Dozen

A dirge will strip the country as the water misses dead men,

The words he dripped were honeyed with the promises of heaven,

Show the soul to shallow ground as ill-fitted as a dollar,

Lo behold a hallowed round that will fit in the revolver,

Near the dam that bled the fane is a lonely wall of coffins,

Here the man he said my name as he showed me all the options,

We get to see the fire from the dry copper pans,

He said I'd be a fighter and that I'd conquer lands,

Split this brick and bomb a soldier if the boys are in the clear,

With his grip upon my shoulder and his poison in my ear,

We mow the blood and lace by a wetter plot of aster,

He showed a dozen fates but I never got an answer,

Still grab the bag and haul ass if we're running down the briar,

We'll crack an egg of knowledge as we're jumping out the fire,

Put the bay leaf to my gum like a pastry to my thumb,

But the baking has begun and he's taping if I run,

Go while blooded to a real tree and you curve into the pedal,

So, I'll cook it and he'll kill me if I burn it on the kettle,

Hide this weapon if a knife cut my rent to hook its rig,

I was threatened with my life, but I went and took the gig.

Invite Only (VIP ~~Plagues~~)

A martyr camps ablaze in the field with the facts,

The card was stamped with lace and was sealed with a wax,

Hand it unopened as a copy like a leshy to the sun,

And the envelope was gaudy but was hefty for a sum,

As rambunctious and amusing as a belt to hold a bag,

The instructions were confusing but they held the only plague,

Paid to hunt the heat and blow up with my toast on the rack,

They instructed me to show up with the clothes on my back,

Cast another thing and hurry if it must be our fears,

As I'm wondering in worry, then this Huxley appears,

Rebelling off the step while we're painting walls and stools,

He tells me not to fret while explaining all the rules,

Wear a car key 'til the sun's up and I pass the blade raw,

There's a party that has come up as a masquerade ball,

We shall be undecided like the money lost to wager,

He tells me I'm invited and the one he wants to cater,

Cut and flagged as clean or corny on a baggy or a bar stool,

But he wagged a finger warning as he dragged me to the carpool,

"In a jail I reap the men and I look through for their gods,

If you fail to meet demand, I will cook you for my dogs."

12.

The Winding Path to Hell

Buy the bacon and the flour with a book to draw it back,

I awakened in an hour while I took a solid nap,

Riots teeming where they see us still in tune with poppy scents,

I was dreaming of arenas filled with food as audience,

To perish in the grave with the knife in my presence,

The carriage was ablaze with the eyes of the peasants,

Bury beggars and their mamas in the years we'll still be by,

Staring daggers through our armors as they pierced the silty sky,

Forty cheers of silly rhyme and the most that you'll read,

For the beers that will be mine like a toast of the mead,

Branding ghosts that will grieve as opposed to their greed,

And we boast that we bleed to the host and his creed,

Fan the coals of the fleet to the toes on their feet,

Dams were closed to the need that arose in the deep,

No one's son is then shot like the death of the wrong boy,

So, we come to a stop with the rest of the convoy,

Though I'll deck out this plum tree like a bear hug to a flower,

So, I stepped out with Huxley as he stared up at the tower.

Serpentine Hallways

Here the facts line the best views like a mallard in a blind,

Where the rats find their refuge in the cellar with the wine,

Cliffs in tandem hold the sun as a band of boulders comes,

It's a mansion overrun like a phantom soldier's guns,

The fires clutch the muddy lye and wear the lungs to cough breath,

The spires touch a bloody sky and tear the tongues of gods left,

Pure as trust that sees us gone with the riches of the others,

Sure as Huxley leads me on to the kitchen and its cupboards,

Pass thy god white as white men on a rosy wall of vices,

As I walk right behind him and he shows me all the spices,

Nearly past the drawer meander in a trial of our age,

"Here we have our coriander by the vial of the sage,

If a sheer dark hovel has the pure-bark palo, then this place is as famous,

In an earmarked bottle is a tear drop model and a taste of our greatest.",

What we're feeding to the flies is bad as action dead ablaze,

Huxley leaves me to devices that he had them set in place,

Dump it out on the fall and dread the waves of a sturgeon,

Hunker down from the hall and prep my space like a surgeon,

Steer this tanker like the rumors that are standing in for truth,

Here I hanker for the humors, but I'm branded for my blues.

A Modicum of Tea and Nothing Else

Chairs that hold special magic are then best to feed the farm,

There's a cold metal jacket that they left to keep me warm,

Bomb the bend from a tower like pay from coke lords,

On the end of a counter that's made of rose quartz,

Fair the city from a hovel as it shook your enemies,

Here I'm tipsy and I topple with the book of recipes,

Fret the funk when I'm buried as I'm clinging to the quake,

Yeah, I'm drunk on the sherry while I'm dreaming of escape,

Throw a fit for the mages when they're scrying awake to fuck,

So, I flip through the pages like I'm trying to make a buck,

Ferrous plumes from a funnel while we fight them with a sick mind,

There was room for a gumbo with the ricin and the strychnine,

Patch the dam dark and breaking when it's cited in the cycle,

As my hand started shaking and decided it was idle,

Must be tended in the tomb like the cribbage as it plays,

Huxley entered in the room with a grimace on his face,

Share my book like a loss with an art that thirsts water,

There I stood and I watched as he barked his first order,

Stay awake in my death, though by then cedars fall,

"Make a cake for my guests so it's ten meters tall!".

Seven Cures

Though I wow the rebels looking, it's the aldermen I sought,

So, by now the kettle's cooking and the cauldron is as hot,

Dip the mages in the cracked pan by a peak that heaven blurs,

Flipping pages like a madman while I seek the seven cures,

Find an antelope for tasting in the pot with pepper set,

I'm an animal that's racing to the god he never met,

Smoke a weed sack and I'm calm as I cuss and eat a shell,

Hoping each act of an alm is enough to keep from Hel,

Force a house in rebellions if their homes hum for poppies,

Forge the boughs of their galleons with the bones from their bodies,

No one takes a buck to break like a failure in the same son,

So, I'll make this fuck a cake and I'll make sure it's a great one,

An old log in the gutter isn't first to fear the riots,

To prolong and to suffer, or to persevere as pious,

Miss that noise and pad the plate like a break for ash prayer,

It's a choice I had to make as I baked the last layer,

Buried money's bloody truth as its charmed boss was sinking,

Therein Huxley stood amused with his arms crossed while thinking,

We tread past a penny to the best tune alive,

He said, "Have it ready when the guests soon arrive!". . .

What I've Become

Nearly buried in a trance - it's as poignant as they now come,

Here I'm staring at my hands, disappointed in the outcome,

Kinda takes me to the sea as I live and look happy,

Mama raised me to be free and to sit and cook candy,

Kissing flowers in the ghetto with the goblets paired and mixed,

It's an hour from the meadow to the cottage where I lived,

Happy wears it out and back then it was that very noon,

Daddy's buried 'round the back end where the blackberries bloom,

All I'm hearing is the bands that will sing their souls for no one,

While I'm staring at my hands, they have means to mold a poem,

Dead awake and sick in thought like the chafing on an asshole,

Let the cake sit and rot while I'm waiting on the casserole,

No one knows if it's a tally pushed like lime in liquor next,

So, I smoke my minutes proudly just to find a quicker death,

Man, I looked to drop like evergreens and breathe the best while dying,

And I stood atop the mezzanine to see the guests arriving,

Hug the wall and avoid what is evil and upended,

From a call to the void to the people that had sent it,

I got comfy on the couch like a khukuri and child,

I saw Huxley in the crowds as he looked at me and smiled.

PART III –
"Catering"

Myopic Miasma

To part back yucks to yield at the creek as we flocked,

The cart had rustic wheels that would creak as we walked,

To call the camp a real view in the sentry's flesh that held it,

The hall was damp with mildew, but my memories meshed and melded,

Lucky shot at a sack lunch and hope for a wish back,

Huxley walked with his back hunched and smoked with his wrist slack,

Time was saving much maybe like we grasped the rebel wars,

I was playing lunch lady as we passed the metal doors,

Come survive an alien feeding fear to teens and God,

From inside the atrium, we could hear the screams abroad,

Hide the dice fierce and full in a rite of the dead,

Like a knife pierced the skull when the night was ahead,

No one brings me to the sheriff like I'm latching down the seals,

So, we sing it to the seraphs and we pass it out in pills,

I suspect they'll need their tests and then vet the vision later,

I expect to feed the guests but am met with prison labor,

Try to lodge them like a coffin if I buried books in back,

I'm exhausted while we walked in and I nearly took a nap,

Fear a factor catching leaders if the books are free in freedom,

Here my captor snaps his fingers and he looks to me to feed them.

Pay Extra for Aesthetic

Lady Rome hid her luck and lime brow, redirected and cloaked,

"They don't give a fuck to find out!", he had said as he smoked,

"See evil's hour one on a hunch to sit next to you,

These people are as dumb as the ones you give credit to!

Find no weather from the land now if ever were a plan or it can't be but a place,

I will never understand how the measure of a man is the candy that he makes.",

In the lap of the future while I break in the Bacardi,

When I snap from the stupor, I awaken to a party,

A virus of the elephants will find us in the shallow ends per bluebloods in there,

The brightness of the halogens in eyelids of an elegance were too much to bear,

Au revoir from bad places with the home known to time the blast,

All I saw were cat faces and a stone thrown at china masks,

Keep on wildin' in a war for men with the blasts at the door,

People smiling were as porcelain as the masks that they wore,

Digging graves to wince in ink with the dig written in dust,

Dripping shades of crimson pink from a lip bitten by lust,

Thursday morn has gray-gold flowers when in lieu of better rum,

Here they hoard their day-old showers like the dew would never come,

Ridding ashes in the sky where the lady buys her luck,

Tipping glasses like a spy but they beg me like a drunk.

Hence the Tiger Eats the Man

Write it raw in the caption like a pill bug by the helpless,

I'm in awe at the mansion that they built up like a palace,

Near the port that man then plays like it's steeple wall ping-pong,

Here the lord of manors reigns and his people all sing songs,

Miss a dead toe on my way through by a truncheon on the gradient,

It's a demo and a prelude to the bumps from in the basement,

Must be miles to my grave if then no one's needing tires,

Huxley smiles and he waves as he's throwing meat to tigers,

It comprised a plan beginning once we do-or-die as men,

I despised the man for many, but I drew the line again!

When the lake boils rays and the fire feasts on land,

Tend the snake oil ways as the tiger eats a man,

Climb back into the main scene from a blunder just as ugly,

I'm snapping from my daydream and I wonder if he drugged me,

Finance the food in flux with the hard clumps of rock,

I never saw it coming,

My hands are glued to rust as the cart comes to stop,

I fed them all to something,

Punching back at the ringers with the red rum to reap us,

Huxley snapped on his fingers and he said, "Come and see this.".

The Man Who Sold the World

We pass the brook's broken bridge and folly at the tomb,

The Master stood motionless and called me to the room,

Hit him violently in batters as he stands down his crime,

Sitting silently in tatters was a man out of time,

Bloody clothes are dropped by people once we steal the nickel vein,

Huxley poked his bodkin needle just to feel a little brain,

A clapback ruling for the dead in a coffin,

The man sat drooling on his bed as we watched him,

To march the muddy row from the blast and the shot,

The cart was running low on the snacks that we brought,

Must be built up to the fringe to reflect the plan's step,

Huxley filled up a syringe to inject the man's neck,

Dread the walls where the dead rot and commute to dam the door,

Dredge the halls like a dreadnought and refute the Man-of-War,

Crusty, crooked cops'd have him like it's hand-to-hand in trouble,

Huxley stood atop as captain and the man began to mumble,

Crunching beer like a bet when we row through the streets,

Huxley sneered as he said, "Let me show you what he eats.",

The damn bridge will rumble while I fret a stone spear,

The man sits and mumbles as he's fed his own ear.

The Lady Without a Face

When insisting it's the carnage once we petrify the swallowed boot,

Imprisoning the artists just to rectify the solitude,

Teach and love the world, fam if it drags and it hurts,

See the doves encircle man as he begs for his nurse,

Dusty baths by the hydrant and we line the sickle's face,

Huxley laughs like a tyrant while we find the fickle cage,

Share no bride with a hundred in the race or the game,

There inside is a woman with the face of a flame,

Bury pits in the convo where the wingless aves found 'em,

There she knits in ensemble as her fingers raise mountains,

Gift the feeble with my whispers on the lanes of another road,

If her needles are the rivers, then her veins are the motherlode,

Playing with a couple crows and saying that it's Lexapro,

Praying to her lover though and hating that she'll never go,

Staying on another note emblazoned from the second row,

Paying for her mother's woe while waiting on her heaven's snow,

Of lately we're a shade of blob like banking on a chaser's taste,

A lady on her way to God in saying that it'd save her face,

Must be birds in the ground if it burns a pellar's isle,

Huxley smirks at my frown as he turns and tells her, "Smile!".

The Boy Dead to Them

Find that custody is see-through as a blast to blow up,

I'm disgusted by the evil and I have to throw up,

Cash will burn and towns will fall if they mind a funny gag,

As I turn to round the hall and I find a fucking crag,

Indecision bears the hit like a pure-breed's mad stare,

In my vision there's a kid and I'm sure he's half there,

Lucky calls unto this place were the marquis and gun,

But he crawls into the space where their stars meet the sun,

Huxley struts to gloat at one, but I pass him up in lesson,

Must be but a noble's son so I ask him but a question,

"Isn't marriage least in love with the graves of each year?

If the parents feast above and the slaves will feast here,

Improved upon an igloo with punishment packing heat,

Then who's the one to feed you, and what is it that you eat?"

A big book of truth just to learn of fake class,

The kid looked amused as he turned to break glass,

"Sear the meat on walks home and the brink of real filth,

Here we eat the hog bones and we drink the swill milk!

Miss my ponies and my pigeons by my bed and end implied,

It's the loneliest existence; I was dead to them alive!".

Objective Catharsis

The vision tethers canned goods so lady luck won't sink,

This mission measured manhood and made me but so meek,

Light the cliffs that sit ablaze on an ancient hill of dead,

Like to give a kid a blade and then make him kill his pet,

Fit the coat tail and sale to your own cell and vale,

Through the death of skies and Annabelle,

It's an Old Yeller tale with the cold cellar ale,

To objectify the chamomile,

Brine chilling in the kettle here as money talks like I sing,

I'm feeling like a predator as Huxley walks like a king,

Barely stamping down a landing from the food and shit he hoists in,

Where he's handing out my candy, but he's doing it with poison!

Bombing Bambi in disguise while we rain all hell for men,

Dropping candy from the skies like he's Gail Halvorsen,

Fear the motherland's defeated in a race to flick the wrist,

Here they cup their hands and plead it for a taste like little Twist,

Hunt the land from a plough here as churches cede cherries,

Dunk the bland in the bough where the birches meet berries,

Mind the old and oaken fae with the candy coal and colors,

Time to mold a broken bay is the sand we stole from others.

Cocooned in Consumption

Clearly some are as sick, very dumb as a twit like an access with a 'B',

Nearly done with this shit; here we come to the ship if the ash is of decree,

Nothing easy brings me fetty as the traps undo the belts,

Huxley sees me breathing heavy and he laughs unto himself,

Bear the banging of the bell like they only bomb the gate,

Therein hanging in her cell was a lonely mom of eight,

Spin the well-rested firs in a darker glade beneath us,

In the cell next to hers was a martyr made of Venus,

Hard as hammers at the handle with the brittle bricks consumed,

Cart cadavers and the cattle to a chrysalis cocooned,

Supreme in crazy shtick by the clocks that we're setting,

The scene will make me sick like to watch a beheading,

I think I may be bit by a wasp that I'm dreading,

To bring a baby crib to the drops while they're betting,

Piss a notion's cup and comp him for the humans that now pray,

It's corrosion up in Compton to the ruins of LA,

Here fentanyl reeks of pain good with the tariffs on the weapons,

Where sentinels seek their sainthood with the seraphs on the seventh,

Pass a step and subtly press its dusty boards on foreign isles,

As I prep to humbly exit, Huxley holds the door and smiles.

.

Lighter Fluid

Lions fed to an angel to defend the wrong countess,

I am led to a table like I tend to longhouses,

Fear abetting what is righteous for the few breaths we sired,

Here and sitting in their silence were the two chefs he hired,

Dusty dew on grass and tongs to taste the land we bombed to death,

Huxley knew their past and wrongs and placed a hand upon their heads,

Playing you for free, pretending it's the lions left on lawns,

Saying, "You could be ascending to the highest echelons!",

Peer at planet peaks in balance with what's built to bring a man in,

Here as panic sinks its talons in the silt that's pink as salmon,

Dusty steps and streets will grieve at the west of wind and peak

Huxley says his piece and leaves as the chefs begin to weep,

Let the greedy drown a tear drop from a tent to take the town,

When completely out of earshot they begin to break it down:

Ask the world if its two old hearts are pounding up a daughter,

As the girl of the duo starts recounting what they taught her,

Test the taste and bomb the city like the helpless town temple,

Says they raised an army quickly as they felt this ground tremble,

Why trust governments with violence if the walls will rend the rook?

I just comfort them in silence as we all begin to cook.

Garum/Posca

Fault the lips and make them mine, but fuck the love to whittle ribs,

Salt the fish and take the time to cut it up in little fifths,

Find the trout drowned behind her where it's tepid and in Krylon,

I'm about out of cider by the exit of asylum,

Dying broke as a pot like my hand will hold ice,

I am coaxed to a stop by the man with no eyes,

Clearly dragging through the rain like a stolen swan of vice,

Here he begs me for a game while he's rolling on his dice,

Fight the fear if death is infinite and set to strip art,

Like you hear an ex's instrument to get your dick hard,

Miss an icon's grave in the rye-rum waves like a sunny hut and real view,

It's a bygone age in a five-bomb blaze as it's coming up to kill you,

Do the kids just ever now see that *Jumanji* is in peril?

Brew the witch's nectar proudly like umami in a barrel,

So, this whole plan of mine will pit an archer to the grave,

Though the old man is blind, his wit is sharper than a blade!

A fuller dose and Swisher when the monk was near a crewman,

He pulls me close to whisper that the monsters here are human,

Pack the fish if in the lake with a candle mount in season,

That to wish for an escape is then tantamount to treason.

PART IV –

"Awakening"

To the Lachrymose Leeches

Dye a raven with a teal sleek and mind the hells that spawn a journey,

I awaken as the wheels creak and find myself upon a gurney,

Halve the fruits for a price in a tent at the lake,

As I move and I writhe and attempt to escape,

A fair sea and ember salt the kings on a pike,

I scarcely remember all the drinks that he spiked,

Buncha birds in the building as the rain will soak in knowledge,

Huxley smirks as he wheels me to the fane of broken solace,

Inaction is a lesson like to show the flare it's glowing,

I ask him but a question and I know it's where I'm going,

"Won't you lead me to the pantry on this precipice we took?

Don't you need me for the candy and the guests for which to cook?"

Share the land's thirty miles burnt with homes in the blaze,

There the man's dirty smile turned to bones like a wraith,

Pass the deathless like it's ball play in a day dad had let us,

At the edges of this hallway with a straight-jacket sentence,

A burning city cupboard in the painting with the war paint,

The gurney flips me upward and I'm hanging from the doorway,

I eat angels with their ribs if nothing nasty is above me,

My feet dangle from the cliffs as Huxley asks me if I'm hungry.

The Sound of Music

A vast and wealthy township that struck the scrimshaw,

The straps they held me down with would rub my wrists raw,

Holy cow and happy Eden in a baggy with a dollar,

Only now they grant me freedom and then tag me with a collar,

Punch a penny in the play once we represent the debts,

Hux had sent me on my way just to reprimand the chefs,

No one's talking if it's all day as it founds a town in duty,

So, I'm walking through the hallway while it drowns the sound of beauty,

Fight their army with a thousand just to read my rhymes to God,

Like a harpy from a mountain as we see the signs abroad,

Spin in panic as it's coming, weighing higher wind we hallow,

In the attic is a woman playing violin and cello,

The queens found my filth like we fucked near no body,

The strings sound like silk when they're plucked here so softly,

To uncertain fate I race 'em each like percolated taste in the copper metal pipes,

A reverberated nation needs a perforated basin so the water levels rise,

I wouldn't invest this movie from the perch through fog and mist,

I couldn't express this beauty for the words do not exist,

Night descends and scares the lonely in a nasty enterprise,

I ascend the stairs unholy as a nascent pair of eyes.

Proof the Ground is Flat

Though I pack my rocks in place, I release it sans a sorry,

Lo I sat and watched amazed like to weave a Stradivari,

Days of beauty lust the nettle in the bane that stands a difference,

They were truly something special in this plane of man's existence,

Know we mettle with prosecco when it only holds the wines,

So, we settle on the meadow when colonial in times,

Piss in panic as I come in like to burn the tree and flesh,

In this attic is a woman as she turns to me and says,

"Eat the snow and act as if it's the trees that stand in water,

Deep below the rabbit's wrath that's beneath the manor proper,

Pears are gleaming in our presence with a seed to cede from doubt,

There's a meaning to this message and you need to seek it out.",

Cook the craw in a place sinking like a sea of ships,

Stood in awe at her grace, blinking while I plead the Fifth,

I'm aware of past of lately in a dream that Death's surviving,

I prepare to ask the lady if she's seen the guests arriving,

Doom a fellow town to ashes when to pack up last in harem,

Soon her cello sounds like scratches on the back of glass and garum,

See the freeze pure in a prism that abides a lonely sky,

She decrees we're in a prison and decides to show me why.

Reinvigoration of the Remnants

Time is haven to the magic like the sage that sat while rotten,

I was taken to the attic to a place he had forgotten,

We maybe fret the pain and grief in hoodies and the face of death,

The lady said her name was Eve and took me to a place of webs,

She wanted costs for war as attack camels came,

Beyond the closet door where the back panels sang,

Miss the part of ya we shift like it's farming on the Rez,

It's like Narnia in myth with their army in the flesh,

I better be go getting head in memory so says the fed,

I've never seen so many dead as enemies go head-to-head,

Leave a holy sea surmounting to inducing free, new albums,

Eve was showing me surroundings, introducing me to outcomes,

I fought the law harder faceless than with masks bleached by sun,

I saw a bard barter pages for his last piece of gum,

Gift this grand weight to the bears that leave the painting as a stallion,

It's a sad state of affairs with Eve explaining their rebellion,

My sons found equal marriage while I made my marriage lethal,

Their once proud people perished and are slave to Herod's evil,

Thieves in pain will see their own soul in a way that cuts a mountain,

Eve explained to me their downfall on the day that Huxley found them.

Around a Campfire Darkly

Crime is leading to a docent like to pack your own pistol,

Time was fleeting for a moment as I sat a stone sigil,

Sickly cats and bone chisels from a stick-up there to market,

Sitting back to hone, whittle, and then pick up where I started,

Chiefs were mapping out the stranding like the evil killed and vanished,

Eve was handing out her candy to the people ill and bandaged,

Kick back Huxley as God as we summon, sow, and plot,

It had struck me as odd that a woman so distraught –

Being burned could beat the cancers like the tenants that sip Jäger,

She in turn would seek the answers to the questions that did plague her,

See the fire and the smoke in the briar by the gate,

She inspired when she spoke and aspired to be great,

Kiss the barley, cull the chaff, and then lift the ice to music,

It was hardly called an act when she risked her life to do it,

Hide a visor with the glove like to head and call the town,

Like a heister for the love when she spread it all around,

Pass the captured crown a wire as the lost leaves combine,

As I sat around the fire and I watched Eve unwind,

Piss a barrel on the summit if a simp can do our part,

It's an arrow in the stomach like a kick unto your heart.

A Story of the Sages

Seem insane to certain stances on the bottom wall of truth,

She explained the circumstances and I brought them all the booze,

Rouse a morning fear to grieve 'specially if it's several thou,

Now according here to Eve, Huxley is the devil now,

Knocks up bellies soft as jelly like to buy a rock from dealers,

Mock a valley's op and deli like to dye a log as killers

No real blow or sacred hit on the grounds or oasis,

So, we'll throw a painted stick at the hounds that'll chase us,

Looking passé and we're cool as another debt to pool in,

Hoping that they are a bull so the color red will fool 'em,

Cut another line and do it like releasing cavalry,

But we're colorblind and stupid when believing that we're free,

'Tis a notion of us dipping while we bank it on the rim,

It's the motion and the whipping of the blanket in the wind,

Beasts are plainly seen in vision if the blast is free to come,

Eve explains to me their mission and then passes me a gun,

Days in bloody snow are due if it's no one's pain to look,

They are running low on food and they know I came to cook.

Salt the Earth Forevermore

Ship the galley to the seas with your own room diseased,

In the belly of the beast like on sow's womb we feast,

I missed the battle and the choir like the weevil left the box,

Amidst the crackle of the fire were the people breading lox,

First, we're muted of our talents as the lords will pick our fights,

Persecuted in the palace and then forced to lick the pipes,

All this time they wore the stigma on this journey that is treasured,

Salty brine is more enigma when you're thirsty as a desert,

Grief was marketing its life from the home it had vanished,

Eve was sharpening her knife with the bone that she brandished,

Burnish patterns with a purpose in the golden light and glass,

Furnish caverns with a furnace as the cold will bite our ass,

Kids are burning in our view from the pantry that's fuller,

Lips are turning to a blue when you can't see their color,

Lift the livery to lowlands and apply a breaking pipe,

It's the misery and moments that imply they're taking flight,

Rope the clothes to the fence as we pluck the flower last,

Coat the coast as you cleanse and we're stuck with sour scraps,

War is homeland and as violent as to be a pack of moose,

For a moment we are silent as we see the shadows move.

A Dance to Remember This

Holy wine that burns the mouth in ascension of the vibes,

Slowly time returns to self as the tension then subsides,

Time to soak the bran and chitlin in the water of the lake,

I'm a broken man and trembling as I ponder my escape,

Ask the leaves past the bran like a Ouija from the last war,

That's when Eve grabs my hand as she leads me to the dance floor,

We're butchering the city in the flesh for the flame,

She looks at me with pity as she says, "You're in pain.",

Icy ground and in a body find the gun that wastes as amply,

I mean, how can I not be, I'm the one that makes the candy!

Dine out dead when I ask for advice that would leave me,

I'm now led where the rats are and rise like a peach tree,

Fear passing through the dark snow in the layman's of the torpid,

We're dancing on the morrow in the matrix of the morbid,

Slant the lock when forcing all them for the souls that risk defeat,

Dance atop the scorching balsam so the coals could kiss our feet,

Duty hasn't called us last and it shows it to begin,

Soon she grabs a ball of ash as she blows it to the wind,

Grass is gray by night and deader snow through the rain and last star,

As I say, "I'd like to get to know you and my name is Gaspar."

Kiss of Undying Cadence

Find a baker for the cruise while we're slaving for the truth,

I'm awakened and confused like I'm breaking in the booze,

Time to take it in to lose when as vacant as the mews,

Shine and shake it from the shoes by the basin in your blues,

Pines are quaking from the grooves when the shape is of your views,

Hide the faces of my muse with the chasers that I use,

Frustrated at the devil and the crone he has to marry,

But I place it in the kettle like a stone and cassowary,

Sheep are flocking to a world where the answers drown the questions,

Eve is watching with a twirl as she hammers out the weapons,

Pennywise eats the heart like the heinous as the heir,

Every strike breathes a spark to the hay that's in the air,

See the towns they filled with shots for the radiance now sundered,

Even clowns are killed for gods with the aliens outnumbered,

Chug Guinness absent from the hand through the fence of a minion,

But in this mansion is a man who condemns in dominion,

Freeze and plaster it in opal in the base of all that isn't,

He's the master and the mogul of this place we call a prison,

Go and face them all in prism past the lighting and decree,

So, we taste the wall and schism as we're fighting to be free.

Brave Old World

Show the sense and shout lower from the air of the moor,

So, the dance is now over to prepare for a war,

Stripping walls of painted pearl with the blue polish ugly,

Tripping balls to save the world like a new Aldous Huxley,

Put the bubbly in a lamp with the fire in the skies,

But the Huxley of this land is a tyrant in disguise,

Show me pain to test the road from a faucet gray as geese,

Only name connects the code and the dots that stay deceased,

Warring plots will take police to the heartless in the fold,

For our thoughts are made of fleece and they warm us when we're cold,

No one missed it if I'm mettled with a bola yanked behind me,

So, I piss it on the kettle and I hold my blanket tightly,

Falling nightly like a baby as my peace abodes a lyre,

All oblige me when I'm angry and I leave my notes to fire,

Kiss the wood adhering only to the tables of a hundred,

With a hood and beard to hold me from the halos that are hunted,

Golden lambs that stay in water like a palace on the trails,

Hold my hand agape to conjure what is calloused as the scales,

Grief is mostly lonely burning cedars so we cool this,

Eve approached me slowly, curling fingers over bullets.

PART V –
"Calamity"

'Tis Better to Live Respected

Trim and trade it if it's simple as an intellect seems,

Inundated by the info and the infrared beams,

Win a bigger bet's cream if the cheddar's ripe in pectin,

Dim the Nicorette dreams and a better life respected,

Chins will check-in in a second on the second rep to bleed,

It's accepted as the next step as we recollect the deed,

Only neck-and-neck indeed as we peck it like a toad,

So, we check the deck to cheat with our Mecca on the road,

Beat the pain and see the people with a posse new and foreign,

Eve explains to me the evil as she walks me through the warrens,

'Tis to saturate the shawarma is to stab it for the boss,

It's exasperated karma and a cackle on the cross,

Throwing tackle to the box with the bait soon to sail,

So, I'm shackled to my loss with escape doomed to fail,

Long to take moons as ale or a virus of Poseidon's,

On a late noon or vale from the sirens to the titans,

Stand in nights living as night is like a pirate's shackled boots,

And my knife isn't as righteous as the silence that'll soothe,

Please defer me to the battle to take money feeling freed,

Eve assures me that it's ample to make Huxley kneel and bleed.

An Insincere Grip

Bleed the story in this copper as an ember slowly packs it,

Greeting morning like a mobster in a members-only jacket,

Gut the bigger bag of bud like we're sick of stacking cups,

Cut the chitter-chatter club with a Bic to back him up,

Punch the kisser past the puck as it puffs leaves as holy,

But the picture matches up with the ones Eve had showed me,

Buried plans to dig from prison shares a hand in missing women,

There the man's astigmatism stares at sand that isn't risen,

Each as surely isn't for her from the finest book of lies,

Eve assures me he's a warrior and that blindness took his eyes,

The candy treats that I win are as calm as in the air,

She grants me leave to find him with a promise that he's there,

Though I'm talking to the magma, it's the islands that are lost,

So, I'm walking through the stigma with my iris on the cross,

Once the righteous knew of gods, it was timeless as the clocks,

Pump the pious through the bogs in the quietest of logs,

Don't invite us to the wash if you stand by defeat,

So, entice us with the mods as the man's eyes would bleed,

Burn the wieners on the bun in the bags of allegory,

Twirling fingers in my palm as he begs to tell his story.

Gramophone of Venus

Eve has served the solo still in like a catcher's rye stays open,

She's the virtuoso villain like a bastardized Beethoven,

Bringing battles to the flag poles and the aforementioned band,

Slinging salvoes at the assholes like the javelins that land,

Fuck the Man and beat the Devil like they're punished due to laws,

Duck the dam and eat the fennel as we rummage through the cause,

Try to smoke him up like Jesus or the burly straps of leather,

I was open to ideas, it was eerie as in ever,

Shut the lid with dead indebted in the dreaded dust of late,

But I didn't get embedded when they whetted us a blade,

In bed, I'd get enraged in pain and shed it like a shepherd's crook,

Instead, I set the stage to flame and readied for my epic look,

I bet it's in the bread or book as crooked as a distant name,

I said it to the second rook and took it to the bishop's fane,

No justice for the civ or sane when systems are a fucking tomb,

So busted that it split its vein and chips in on a bloody moon,

Where we must be by the bone in the bagged leaves of music,

There's a dusty microphone and I begged Eve to use it,

Peaks will plummet to the broken in descents that parse a wing,

She's reluctant for a moment but relents and starts to sing.

Bar Singer Fire Water

Bind the mercy to the tallow as we come in for the scene,

I'm unworthy to the hallowed and this woman is a queen,

Beaches bomb a bay with bubbles and the noise of God's laugh,

She's the calm away from cuddles with a voice like soft glass,

Slow the row of such tasks from the mast to the sail,

So, I know I must pass like a class that I failed,

Ice to cool it if you live in pain and kick it with a bit of shame,

Bite the bullet that we dip in paint and chip in to the slit or vein,

The ticket is the hidden crane that picks it like a recent puddle,

A picket like for chickens slain to live it like you're Regan Russell,

Bidding every price and law on this newly crafted story,

Sitting mesmerized in awe from the beauty cast before me,

Much to whet and sharpen blades from the sum of all defeats,

But the debt is far from paid when they come to call receipts,

I submit my broken bogie to the golden brook of heaven,

I just sit and smoke a stogie that I rolled from book and resin,

Send a sack paid to rats on the hardest day to hold,

In this shack made of thatch, but my heart is made of coal,

A time when apart depends on help for these things,

The rime on my heart begins to melt when she sings.

Flamey the Candle Mandrake

I've been bailed from land and pressed it where a test bomb lies,

I then held her hand a death grip like a DEFCON 5,

Torn like film if from a genius where the pain writhes in woe,

Form a kiln from in my fingers where the flame hides to grow,

Show the fools a dunce mind is 0 for 2 at crunch time,

Sober truths in lunch lines are overused as punchlines,

Sow the roots in much lime as donors lose their sunshine,

So, we do this such rime if no one's noose has touched mine,

Throw this shit at a business as the same pistols pout,

So, I sit back and witness as the flame fizzles out,

Some explosions are of cars with the sounds that spurn the bells,

From implosion of the stars to the towns that burn like wells,

Some will ask us if we're for this from the seat just soaked and slain,

From the ashes of the Torus is a creature roped in flame,

Whiff the civil soldier's sea breeze as it tiptoes from the spire,

It's a little over three-feet as it skips rope with the fire,

Wear a whittled wing of focus with the sand bags to stand me,

There this little thing approaches as its hand begs for candy,

Book this breeze in the port like the miles on a tug,

Look to Eve for support as she smiles with a shrug.

Smelt the Spelt & Whiff the Chaff

Pristine as pants and new fleek on a timid student beach,

This thing it stands on two feet and it mimics human speech,

Teach the flame a separate flute like the omens hiding pentagrams,

We remain as resolute as the Romans writing epitaphs,

Show a brittle cedar last if it's the trunks that last the rain,

So, this little creature dances as it jumps and asks my name,

Nice, new step – instead it pays like the league in my pocket,

I move back to give it space with intrigue like a rocket,

Pass the god less when you drop it like the conscious cunts we found,

As it shocks us from the cockpit and then launches us aground,

Catch the goblin, lich, and hound if the weight is then this heavy,

Ask the coffin, shift the sound, and then wake us when we're ready,

Bits of zany trust in our deal with this candle and his flames,

Little Flamey does a cartwheel as he cackles and explains,

"Line their targets with a weapon tense and cunning cracks to see through,

I'm an artist in the present sense that's coming back to free you."

Time is staking stacks of lives on a grain of sand and spittle,

I was taken back surprised as the flame began to fiddle,

Peace that says the meadow's lively as the man made his sighting,

Eve then preps her rebels lightly in this sad state surviving.

A Lamb Hunting Lions

This devil hooked the bras slumbering next to a dungeon

The rebels took applause numbering less than a dozen,

Raw trust and flame swords where they teach what men are bad,

Sawdust was main course like the Siege of Leningrad,

Share a sighting of the blade like it's King Tut's head,

There was rising from the grave like a mink once dead,

Terror finding that we're saved from the things mum said,

Bear this side when of the raid if we drink rum red,

Throw the book and crooked rock at the damn baby swallow,

So, I stood and took a walk as I had Flamey follow,

Dumping out the bombs on town faced with names sick of need,

Touching down upon the ground makes the flames pick up speed,

A preacher that's insidious as the date that he wants,

The creature is oblivious to the fate that it flaunts,

Sherry toasts are chump change to a grudge and adieu,

There are those that snuff flames like a smudge on their shoe,

Dig my blades a real turnip if the money's now cool,

It's a place of ill worship and it's Huxley's crown jewel,

Hoard the gold and diamond ash in the depths of the division,

Lord behold the shining path as I prep for an incision.

The Marquis Deveraux

Sipping grapes from aquifers with the macarons to nourish,

Gripping blades like banisters in the catacombs of courage,

Only saved from the loss when it pays what we please,

So, we blaze on the cross with the graves that we grieve,

In honor of the lathes and limb when thought to toss them shotgun shells,

The manor was a maze of men from top to bottom posca shelves,

Bloody when we're captured to afford the death and scene,

Huxley was enamored by amor and mezzanine,

In the wars we elevated on green grass and the waters,

And the floors were separated between staff and the squatters,

Wall the dove in death it's meeting as it sees the bars it bent,

All above the guests were eating at a feast with hearts content,

Reach the molding of the body as they join in to the max,

Eve was holding on a shotty as she pointed through the cracks,

The sight that sates its listeners comes to bite the plate of integers,

The light escapes like prisoners just to fight their fate at distant firs,

Only night to play with shit to stir and rites to sway a wizard's hearse,

So, we shy away what did occur and slice the way with scissors first,

The hardiest dad would still doubt if it's steady and it hurt,

The party has had their fill now so they ready for dessert.

Certain Death Shall Follow

Mr. Madness is the main thing as this book rose with a rhyme,

It's a canvas that I'm painting in the footnotes of my mind,

Huxley's henchman is a high risk and is hollow as a gourd,

Plus, he benches what I'd die with if I followed him to court,

This is them, the dead with purpose and their view to take commands,

Mr. M has met the servants and refused to shake their hands,

Pick the same robin's nest from the earth to its absence,

Picture Dwayne Johnson mixed like with Lurch from the Addams,

If the fans show the mob as their hands go to God with a lasso on top,

It's a dance so macabre that the plants sow their plot with the gnats so they rot!

Jack the witness near the car so they pay me like a soldier,

Back to business, here we are, and there's Flamey on my shoulder,

I support no street shopping as I'm forcefully robbing,

It's abnormal eavesdropping as that portal keeps stopping,

Maybe chip the bits of ice as the hapless stay sober,

Flamey gives me his advice as the Madness takes over,

Coming from a tomb of dogs like an earthen crow disguised,

Something in the room is off as the vertigo arrives,

Bear the burden free of buying in the silence of the hills,

There's a certainty arising from the irises and ills.

A Great Leap Forward

Why give me bigger bichirs past no city big as lemurs?

My itchy trigger fingers have so simply picked their ringers,

Buy a midnight flotilla by a pickle that we choose,

Like a fish-fry vanilla with a nickel in the blues,

Can the fishies from the cruise with a leak that spread for weeks,

Man, it's dripping on my shoes while I speak and prep my speech,

Find my sound, must apply to walls at depths as some split it,

I'm like Mao justifying all the deaths that come with it,

Crumbs are cooking if we're late to the kettle when it lies,

But I'm looking at my blade like a devil in his eyes,

Stand in grass and lost of lately with leaves' pungency to wreak,

And I ask the gods to save me as Eve nudges me to speak,

I hear the ode in monsters' deaths and seek to pawn the legion's seal,

I clear my throat of conscious threats and keep it on an even keel,

To bother us and check no prison clothes amidst the dirt,

The squatters and the rebels listen close to hinge the word,

No one makes it out the alley if we missed and threw the dye,

So, I say it loud and proudly with a fist unto the sky!

"Lucky rings entrust the rebels with the gems of vault and urn,

Huxley thinks of us as pretzels that he bends to salt and burn."

PART VI –
"Banality"

The Roswell Resurrection

By a road spitting swill with a crank as it sealed,

I awoke sitting still on the bank of a field,

Wooden bells and bikes that lock from the shed as they push us,

Couldn't tell the sky from rock as it bled to the bushes,

My December's fake and scraggly as I look like shit or feral,

I remember making candy and then cooking it per kettle,

Run amok hidden through this sour luck thick as Gatlin,

What the fuck did I do and how the fuck did it happen?

Lilacs for deaths of OGs and a set step to catch,

My hands are pressed as posies and the bed head to match,

Seeing smoke to rein in chains like a trade road in Greece,

Even clothes I came in changed to a plaid robe of fleece,

I plan to make it talk to my edda's faded floors,

I stand and take a walk through this meadow made of orbs,

Chew the guanabana's taste while lounging like a can of nuts,

Blue as Araucana eggs and bouncing like a planet does,

Swoon the seated by the cedar in the rings of the table,

Soon I'm greeted by a reaper with the wings of an angel,

It's the big blades and dose to douse the house or rut like Odin,

With his rib cage exposed, he now espouses what is broken.

52.

Judgement of the Damned

Tie this rope to bring in kills from the heavens I shall heat,

I awoke to screaming hills and the peasants night will eat,

Spoon the cream to blend what's in it with the dead end's dry storm,

Soon my dream was then upended by the pendant I'd worn,

Near the cedar's melting ice was the timber dead and lonely,

Here, the reaper held his scythe as he bent his neck and told me,

"Quite the sights for the value like they're bids to bring before me,

I'd oblige what I tell you if you wish to see the morning."

Though I'd cop it if it's cool, this was hiding it in beauty,

So, I nodded like a fool that was pirating a movie,

Seeing soft porn now in class was a date to rest and make love,

Eating popcorn out the ass while we wait for death to take us,

Stand on real ice for the team like its death takes the timely,

And I realize it's a dream with my best days behind me,

Throwing blows to prize defending timely smiles strong as sight,

So, I close my eyes pretending I'm a child on his bike,

Try to center ash per pitfall as suns set and die too,

I remember as a kid all the fun shit that I'd do,

Sow the phlox at the stream as I burn in Hell at forty,

So, I toss in my dream as I turn to tell a story.

Cookies & Cream

Top us up to stay the plan as drama dusts a burning world,

Papa was a labor hand and mama was a working girl,

Shit the comers that'd came in to this crazy old town,

It was summers in the basement when our AC broke down,

Don a fad and slay the kills to off the cuff's incumbent cool,

Mama had to pay the bills since papa was a drunken fool,

Part the reins now for tort like your honor made us smile,

Cart the claims down to court with the proper papers filed,

As he aisle-rushed the bailiff and he shunned a victim mind,

Daddy smiled 'cause he came in with a gun they didn't find,

Paid to sit by when it's over with a sip from our own barrel bung,

Made 'em strip like it was poker and he hit like Charles Harrelson,

Brawn is bred for bust and mural and decried by a crier,

Mama said he was a hero and he died in a fire,

Fit the noose to cut journeys to the earliest of quotas,

But the truth is no such mercy in the dirtiest of photos,

Dot the dust and lonely home if trauma loves a loss so seldom,

Papa was a rolling stone and mama was the moss that held him,

I test my death so some come learn the tides I'd swum that sit awake,

I guess they left no stone unturned besides the one that skipped the lake.

Wild Ones Run Barefoot

Spin the scheme's shares to split and a spool of sins to sate the imps,

In my dreams there's this kid that'd fool his friends to paint a fence,

Kinda riled from the scent like the piled dung and crap,

I'm a child once again and a wild one at that,

Strip the tents like a tire as we're showing love to shiver,

With my friends for a fire while we're going up the river,

Both our pockets filled like faucets with a colander's compliance,

Nostradamus killed the cautious with a calendar for Mayans,

Though we seldom hear the silence, it's the caution's that we kill,

So, we salvage fear and violence from the flotsams in the spill,

Half our whole lives ripping off and shifting sands for night and ode,

As a boy I's skipping rocks and kicking cans with kite and code,

Seal the candle wicks and say that they're kind enough to call,

Building battlements with clay where we line 'em up to fall,

Ship the sand to fill the ring for the day rigs will freeze,

Kick a can to kill the king while we play 'Pigs & Thieves',

Time for living in a second like a two-toast chickadee,

I'm reliving what I reckoned on a roof so rickety,

Pour my own gin and retire skill to cut the lines of freedom,

For a moment I see fire 'til they shut the blinds of Eden.

Lowkey at the Orchard Gate

Sort the gold and bomb them back like the fuzz is in the rear,

Lord behold the common gnat as he buzzes in my ear,

Block the ride and auto mountain in a clean race for fun,

Walk beside the marble fountain and the dream tastes of rum,

Chug the SoBe jugs and mixture with the rime and rugged 'round it,

But I'm lowkey just a trickster with a dime the dozen doubted,

Mix the mind with mush to mount it like the wars that need a weapon,

It's the grime and snuff surrounded with the doors that lead to heaven,

Right as embers candled shivers with a common noose and stake,

I remember apple fritters that my mama used to make,

Live like Babe Ruth and bunt it to admit you're bold as most,

Given slave food as comfort and comfit to cull the coasts,

No one fits the golden clothes like a foreign inch decided,

So, submit to hold the toasts at the boar and bridge ignited,

There is more to stench I cited on the treasure's latch and tome,

Where a boorish wench is sighted in the deserts cast from stone,

With my garbled canvas sacred as the grainy gate and rut,

If a marble cactus made it, then we maybe made the cut,

Crashing into moose and fine bucks as a menace paints his pantry,

As I'm introduced, a time flux makes horrendous changes lastly.

Connection for the Forlorn

Mama mashed and stoked the conscience with her angels killed for fun,

Trauma grasps the throat of progress and it strangles 'til we're done,

Stares are tethered to the canvas as they break the codes like genes,

There's a method to the madness to mistake for modes and means,

Doughy clay will soak the seams if it holds the post he bided,

So, we prey on broken dreams with a golden coast ignited,

Knowing most are host to hide it in the streets of olden towns,

Though we do-si-do and cite it as our means to mold the mounds,

Miss the fragger in the crater as a shepherd in a saga or a storm in the present,

It's so mega with the Maker and as meta as the data when forlorn in connection,

Some go flush from the panic once they're found in the tub,

Knuckle dust in the attic; buck 'em down in the club,

Cook the town in the mud if it's really part of life,

Look around for the blood and you feel you are alive,

Kisses kill you with the eyes like a curfew at a dusk,

If it builds you from the ice and it burns you to the dust,

But you pursue what is lies as you yield to sin and leisure,

What you search through is the skies as you feel the synesthesia,

Go feel the men that eat ya when you're made into a portrait,

So, distill the gin beneath ya and awaken to your torture!

Suffer for the Art of Self

Made in pairs still with doom as you pop it back in place,

Vacant stares fill the room like a toxic gas escapes,

We break in while escaping prison when the tour's down a tractor,

Awaken to a fading vision and the hoarse sound of laughter,

Try dirt plots firs evaded from the gnarliest of armpits,

My first thoughts were invaded by an army of this darkness,

Itchy carpet in the office cut and let out near the crew,

Since we started and accomplished what we set out here to do,

Once the truth assails inward, then it sounds like it's an option,

From the screws and nails interred in the grounds like they're a coffin,

No one cut the facts to powder like the victim of a trolley,

So, I pluck the scabs a flower and I flick 'em in my folly,

Shit, I'm salty as a relish as they run through and they chase men,

Sick and jolly in my malice as I come to in the basement,

Riding hunger past the creature like a lummox hunter comes unfit

I've been under anesthesia and I wonder what this someone did,

Muddy pants and slop adore me when I'm reeking through the door,

Huxley stands atop a story and I'm peeking through the floor,

Send a team to the wild when they clean like a clock,

In my dream I'm a child and the cream of the crop.

Rusty Clocks Stop Ticking

Try to stick 'em with a gun when they're breaking in to guard us,

Like a victim of a bomb that is waking to the carnage,

In an opera seat we stop the show's oddity ultimately fleeing,

An anomaly, the nominal probably awkwardly breathe freely,

Such as dragons steal the gold with their luck to weigh a wing,

Rust the wagon wheels of old as we pluck a fraying string,

Put your balls up in your mug and not feel the same in pride,

But nostalgia as a drug cannot kill the pain inside,

It's atonement when we wake up with a smile fit for pogos,

It's a moment that we make up as we file it with photos,

Freedom from the harbor's waste, people bring and bait it wrong,

Even in the darkest days we will sing our favorite song,

Mist the yarrow and the river when you're standing on the crocs,

It's an arrow in a quiver and a phantom on the phlox,

No surrender, not for fake love like the faceless at the gallows,

So, remember what we're made of in this matrix of the mallows,

Shade the yellows in a gray cup so the ministries go follow,

Made to mellow men so made up in their images so hollow,

No geese or flock defeat the dock that needs its rock to smoke or cook,

So, grease the clock at three o'clock to meet the god that wrote the book.

Water Wings

Shine a brighter beam in open skies with fiery wings and broken ice,

I'm a time machine to close my eyes on ninety things that spoke of lies,

Die an ember in an alley with a dollar for the copper,

I remember mama held me as a toddler in the water,

Tack the metal in the cupboard as I up and leave the gin,

Wrapped in nettle and the mugwort at a coven tree of sin,

Such as fate suffers oddly from a pitcher in a glass,

But the blaze touches softly on my picture with the ash,

Stand in mud and know the weather as you pick a scene to leave us,

And I rub it slow as ever with a cig between my fingers,

Strong as sauce in homes that last from the bucket to the builder,

On the cross to own the blast as I puff it to the filter,

Rushing bodies to the waters like they're tapirs in their build,

Pushing poppies to the poplars with the bakers in the field,

Too absurd to say the plan and overt to state the stand,

We procure a day of ham and don't stir this plate of jam,

It's the soot clouds on a body as the covens hide the kill,

It's the cookouts mama taught me that my cousins tried to steal,

Try a sure thing like a soldier if your mama looks happy,

I was thirteen when I told her I was gonna cook candy.

A Crystalline Kaleidoscope

Paint is calling to the clown to climb and step into soliloquy,

Faint from falling to the ground like finding heaven at a Dollar Tree,

Come in once you've succeeded with abundant gusts in there,

But my lungs have receded and they're pumping dusty air,

I'm alive and I feel it as I look around the room,

Time to die when I kill 'em and I cook this town in doom,

Try the nights for their thunder like my covers pad the vain book,

I survived but I wondered if the others had the same luck,

Gift the gold, pearls, something, to their old devil racket,

It's a cold world coming in a full-metal jacket,

Send the smoke on in to hack it when you break it like a lock,

And I hope some men will back it when I take it to the top,

Damn the quaking, ticking clocks if to fade a penny's thoughts in a poem,

And I'm breaking city blocks on their vacant, gritty rocks when I throw him,

Die waiting for the petals to then sunder what's created,

I'm aching for the rebels but I wonder if they made it,

Past the broken peace as ageless as the fence by the road,

As I go to leave the basement and then whence, I awoke -

The one that fears demise is the schnook that Death will fear,

The sun had seared my eyes as I took a breath of air.

PART VII –

"Ellipsis"

Laconic in Bathos

Down and out in fading moments where the pain plants feelings,

Now my mouth is hanging open like a hanged man's ceiling,

Here the same dam's filling through the forests sharing clothes,

Where the rain lands really, do we know it's where it goes?

No one dead will come around me as the wall burned the ground,

Though my head is fucking pounding and I'm all turned around,

Say I wandered to their camp and I said it was Orwellian,

Yeah, I wonder where I am and remember the rebellion,

Pass a book and then the plan with the thankless crux we nourished,

As I look into my hand that is caked with dust and courage,

Ban the bud and bake the bread list when they back it up with beer,

And the blood escapes a crevice as I lap it up in fear,

Shun the sock when I taste it as a mirror screens a meadow,

From my spot in the basement, I could hear the screams in echo,

In the back go stepping softly to the bluer pad and light,

And I had no weapon on me, but I knew I had to fight!

Tasks that run through in our future are the kind risks will leave,

As I come to from my stupor and my mind shifts to Eve,

I am here to taste their deaths in the water like my rum,

I prepare to face the guests as the monster I've become.

Scraps of Leftovers

I respect a sea of great men like an Ent of garden heirs,

I expect to see a banquet but am met with ardent stares,

Dare to dodge guns now triggered like the cradles on their shields,

Where the spots once held silver on the tables with the tilts,

Count the evil heirs to bomb as their cases haunt a sibling,

Now the people stare in calm with their faces gaunt and shifting,

Cocky grins could see a hundred wins in violence hacked away,

Dropping pins would be redundant since the silence stacked the hay,

Past the stables steeped in hardships and the horse homes they rouse,

As the tables reek of garbage and the pork bones they house,

Stab a shadow cloaked in black and an ancient lich today,

And the camel broke his back from the games in which we play,

Pass the dangers split for days like a day abroad for children,

As the faceless hit their trays and they pray for God to kill them,

Highest up the grimy wall when hounded by the dead soldiers,

I was in the dining hall surrounded by their leftovers,

Au revoir for trust resuming from the fires of the chosen,

All I saw were husks of human and survivors of the poison,

Dusty book and lock are helping me for miles in the river,

Huxley stood atop the balcony and smiled for his picture.

Get 'Em Good

I should be the golden dye parched and worn like bloody shtick,

I could see an old goodbye arched to burn in Huxley's grip,

Nasty wood will rot with everything by no parking in the lot,

As he stood atop the mezzanine while barking like a dog,

Let's hoist a pool of censors to the open gate and cell,

His voice was full of tremors, but he spoke of hate and hell,

Spawn an ode I gave to self like I checked the boxed juice,

On the road that's paved to tell as he let them dogs loose,

Set to step and not move like I'm running from my shadow,

Let the weapons drop truth if I'm coming in my camo,

Stand on something like a castle or a moat with rocks at ease,

And I'm gunning for this asshole, so I hope he stops to breathe,

As I sow this thought to freeze on the rugged seas sailing,

And I know he's not police, but the fucker keeps wailing,

Dusty borders doubt the bend and an anthem of the kids,

Huxley ordered out his men as he sent them to the Styx,

Hum the plot where they all stay with good beer and devils dreaming,

From my spot in the hallway, I could hear the rebels screaming,

Show the step too steep to do, though the floors say it's a peak,

So, I prep to peek a boo through the doorway as I creep.

Cuerno de Chivo

Thy madness doesn't go far with its grind as it's risen,

My hand is on the crowbar with my mind on the mission,

Dry semen on a candle wet to ape it when we spread the shot,

I'm creeping with a vandal step and make it to the heaven spot,

Calls are kidding with a laugh in an ode of calming cinders,

Walls are splitting with the cracks to explode the rotting splinters,

Dripping profits from their malice with their deaths or fall debated,

Sipping sauces from a chalice and the guests are all sedated,

Die while talking to the corvids as they noose the diction's lie,

Like I'm walking through a forest with the crucifixions nigh,

No recruits will give goodbyes in the plating of the hall,

So, we shoot the shit to sky while we're waiting for the fall,

Such as trading for a ball in distinction of the jobless,

But the mating in its call is extinction of the thoughtless,

Plus, we victims are a coven and the guests pressed are our vices,

Huxley did 'em by the dozen and he left them to devices,

Destined lessons share what sight is with the truth to feel as godly,

Mesh their deaths in where the night is and they choose to kill us softly,

Cutting down a floor and candle when I throw this rhyme at dead men,

But I'm out the door and ammo as I go to find a weapon.

The Torture of a Butterfly Wing

The camera was assessed as then the piss ant had won,

The manor was a cesspit and a death camp in one,

Show 'em if something's fine to press the finger's fallen stone,

No one in their fucking mind would ever think to call it home,

Nothing new as all and ever that would pad the wall for winter,

Huxley fooled 'em all to get here and then had them all for dinner,

Miss the bad tide and knee like I can't find my team as I seek their gold plating,

It's a sad irony in the pad by the sea when I keep it cold gravy,

Cut the key that's so shady, dipped in weed scents and vibes,

But I need to know baby, did my Eve since survive?

Risk a peace rinsed like rice on the deep and crackling drawl,

It's the trees hinged to life as I peep a cracking wall,

Why appear to end their mocking by a sea of deader trees?

I could hear their men are talking; I could see they're enemies,

We're rebuffing what we're viewing with an icy-jacket option,

They're discussing what they're doing with their nicely packaged toxin,

Shunning crowds like prison laws as they stop to sip what's sold,

Unannounced and given cause as I'm watching it unfold,

Dusty grain will stain their outfits from the message to their mouths,

Huxley came to paint the town red in the visage of himself.

Dirty Grapes Ablaze

Grainy rain on the grapes that adhered to the lie,

Flamey came from the drapes and appeared in the sky,

Calm the soldier on the table when desire is a bitch,

On my shoulder was an angel with the fire of a lich,

As I dick about and stammer where an ego finds its eyes,

As I looked around the manor for a single sign of life -

Sip a beer and test the TV as they race to God to grieve,

It was clear that Death had beat me to the place I sought to siege,

Take me back across the stars to the old me's fucking spot,

Flamey sat and crossed his arms as he told me what he thought,

"Dart your eyes to the pad and the launch it surrounds,

Carbon cries when it's sad as the conscience allows,

Chuck your dice and cut a song book as you fade into the soft sky,

What is life if but a construct that we make into colossi?"

Make me sell my land in peace with a god or friend to fall,

Flamey held my hand at ease as I thought to end it all,

Blood the shade of rose and canvas like the paint of pride or PD,

But I made the most of madness as it came and tried to eat me,

Shit won't faze me save for lies in the new weeks of calm,

Little Flamey gave advice and then poof, he was gone!

Build a Stairway to Heaven

I want to build them thanks and then sell it where the wine was,

Gel is in the fizz now,

I walk the pilfered planks by the pallet of the pine nuts,

Tell it like it is now!

Moving faster than y'all, here to lead the trail of life,

Through the cracks in the wall where I see this hell alive,

Garish authors are creating what is golden in a black light,

There's a monster in the making, but they mold him like a crack pipe,

Drink the tears that dawn a cradle teeming with the best of great men,

He appears upon the table screaming for his death to take him,

Grief in hand when luck is not like the craziest of sons,

He's a man they plucked abroad from the shadiest of slums,

Smite them all and ten-day quota for the panic it was stopping,

Like a call from MKUltra and the acid they were popping,

Shock the mind if feeling sad when like a peacock cut to hue,

Block the blind from building bad men when they see not what they do,

Bloody battles on a bad end are deprived of Earth's blood,

Huxley cackled like the mad men and incised the first cut,

This wisdom seemed before us as a slight to seven cedars,

His victim screamed a chorus that could light a heaven's heaters.

There's a Gauntlet of Forgotten Souls

Heavy metal to the mask and lead the dread when in flames,

Every rebel that I passed was either dead or in chains,

Rocky pigeons and a pink dove cut the curtain when it's ample,

Not existence that is dreamed of, but a burden like a black hole,

Time to die and pray to God as they plead for breathing rites,

I'm alive but they are not, and I see their bleeding eyes,

Must be silly shit for somewhere or the evil in the back end,

Huxley really did a number on the people that attacked him,

Seed the world if it's always in its winter at the harbor,

He encircled in the hallways and he pincered in the parlor,

Keep your distance in the village if you dread the law for something,

Blink and miss it if you're privileged but you never saw it coming,

Know we're bonded to the fellows like the hottest coals we heated,

Throw the gauntlet to the gallows where forgotten souls will lead it,

Ties for talk if handed ice with a pick and caving peak,

I's a modest man in life, but this shit has made me weak,

Dusty steps and day-old zen to mist the windless song for feels,

Huxley's left a trail of men and Mr. M is on my heels,

Leaves are drifting to the creak past the beer and bogs or bunting,

Eve is missing and I'm weak as I hear their dogs are coming.

Mist to Madness

To salt fish like a bath and see no man offer first,

This hall is like a path between Roman aquifers,

Tasting like the titty that's concerning while we order up,

Blazing when the city's sacked and burning in the corner pub,

Miss a friend's body signing when befriended by an Aztec,

Mr. M saw me hiding and ascended to the last step,

Resentful of the matters that could make the days as better,

The temple is in tatters – and the takeaway, whatever!

Swish the gin clutched to crawl as they all hate the world,

Mr. M touched the wall and the wallpaper curled,

Carve a fist in his tomb to lift the pen past the bloke,

Carbon kissed on the moon like Mr. M as he spoke,

"If I'm torn from what's true, then it's once we conned the don,

This the thorn in the shoe that Mr. Huxley wanted gone?"

Time is older than a test if it picked him from a glass,

I was holding in my breaths like the victim of a crash,

Come for me – they're now mourning – this the end cooked in love,

Suddenly without warning, Mr. M looked above,

Twist a cap to the cleaners that had dirt on his skin,

With a snap of his fingers and a smirk to his grin.

It's a House of Twisted Horrors

Hear the sound if of amendments like the Devil tatted God's skin,

Here they rounded up the remnants of the rebels that'd wronged him,

Ejected from a mouth so bloody, fallen thoughts are bleeding from it,

Except in the House of Huxley, all the gods are being hunted,

With the corniest of missions and a plaque to fix the road,

It's inglorious decisions to enact the twisted code,

Going back to pick the rose as I sack their tent and hell,

So, I practice shit in droves and I hack the flint to sell,

Such is satchels split like cells with their Santa fit to freeze,

But it's accurate to tell that I can't comfit to please,

And he had to grip the trees as he sat somewhere and seized,

As he racked up sitting fees and they tacked a fare in threes,

That's a pack of TNT and a jack compared to queens,

No one shows up for their freedom if they kiss their hell and fail,

So, it blows up and it beats 'em as they live to tell the tale,

I am bandaged and am bait with this scent on my skin,

I had managed to escape Mr. M on a whim,

Pinch my pen in my sin with times turning to a temple,

Ten eyes in from the wind with lies whirling like a petal,

Since I's 10 with my kin and I's stirring with the kettle.

PART VIII –
"Requiem"

I, the Army Against Myself

Every crime will credit fair fucks for their fame and body dragging,

Barely time to exit air ducts when they came and caught me slacking,

Timeless thimbles are as fraught as a bog from its dregs,

I was nimble and was caught like a frog for its legs,

Musky wetlands smell as lively as a pack of dollar smokes,

Huxley's henchmen held me tightly as they snapped the collar closed,

Tannins tanned to cull the oaks deemed to lie on the stone steps,

And it's sad but all the folks seemed to die in their own ~~deaths~~,

Shit, I mean in their own beds, and even then, it's highly suspect,

Should I see what I know next as freedom's friend and nightly nut check?

Time to strip him like he's halls that would spread the sheet between,

I could kick 'em in the balls, but could never keep it clean,

Miss the Earth as it plummets with the words of the sonnets,

It's a curse and a promise like a birth of the comets,

Gases burn through the progress of a day 3 as well,

As they burst through the concepts and they drag me to Hell,

They will murder me in habit in the way ale makes a brew,

They refer to me as 'Rabbit' and they say they'll stake a stew,

Day by days is dim as mummies like to stack the dead in file,

They appraise my limbs for monies, but they grab my head and smile.

Squish the Keys

Time is bagged weed for getting by to half cock on the whole man,

I was dragged deep and kicking by their laptop with the program,

I hope you all are bound and hard up for their stupefied indifference,

The jovial sound to start up with computerized assistants,

Knowing new skies are limits for the mortar laid in ash,

So, if you can rise within this, then they'll know you're made to last,

Court a quart of 'caine and grass as we paint him in our etchings,

Pour the war on grain and glass as we thank 'em for our blessings,

Skies are throwing down a number of a certain play and game,

I was zoning out from hunger when I heard it say my name,

Only god that's dead to book club is the bird that devils fling,

Slowly cocked my head to look up at the dirty little screen,

Pair the handsy with the bygone if they broke it like it's wobbly,

There and dancing was an icon as he floated like a body,

Eat the world in a while from the top bunk or bed,

He was purple with a smile as his thought bubble said,

"Hi, my name is Squishy and I see you are enslaved!

Buy my ageless whiskey if you reach too far in rage,

I should write a value called 'quits' if you'll cheat and show your pain,

I would like to help you solve this, but I need to know your name!"

Employee Training Video

Stay back around behind me like it's putty in my stubbly hair,

They sat me down and tied me and then put me in this fucking chair,

Trained to rise up in my dream that I used the eco yeast in,

Aimed my eyes up at the screen in this Ludovico treatment,

Very deadly as a crash like we burned the CD's song,

There they left me as they laughed and they turned the TV on,

Since we nut up as we scream, it's what's slaughtered in this instance,

Squishy jumped up at the screen and he offered his assistance,

Flush anew with such relief like cunts for titillated dicks,

Much ado to clutch a reef and punch a pixelated fish,

Fishy mountain in the valley and the pass is as essential,

Squishy's bouncing and he's happy as he acts as existential,

"I'll be here in the flesh, though I'll pass down what I held,

I see you're in distress, so I ask how can I help."

Go in hiding with a care and a second wave to rouse,

Though they tied me to the chair, they had never taped my mouth,

Show up knocking for a fiend like to buy low as we ball,

So, I'm talking to the screen like a psycho to a wall,

Torn from reed to burn the blend as they heard from all of us,

Born to bleed and merk the men with this purple octopus.

Clipping Through Environments

Perpetually I'll be the man that digs his house with wine sealed,

Eventually I freed a hand to click the mouse for *Minefield*,

Smiles forbidden and are ridden from the midden to the tomb,

While I'm sitting as a victim and am hidden from the room,

Press your prick into the plume when you're dicking through the fall,

Yes, I'm sickened and I'm doomed like I'm clipping through the wall,

Chug the sicko sanction's smoothie as you miss me in the mirror,

But the simple actions soothe me and it's Squishy that I fear,

Prints I took will give their lives from a battered eye and bone,

Since I look to live alive, but I'd rather die alone,

Fifty miles to the stream like the braves will slow the bridle,

Squishy smiles on the screen that he saves from going idle,

It's a mask of the bishop as he laughs at the laws,

It's a dash of militia in a crash with the cause,

It's a blast and a mix-up with a gash in the paws,

It's the last that we lift up when they bash on our flaws,

Cities seedy, sick, and separately the skies will ease them open,

Squishy sees me click incessantly and tries to seize the moment,

Pass the brook and the stream simply if two are blind,

As I look to the screen, Squishy says, "You are mine.".

77.

Cobble's Knot

Why fear the dungeon in the nights if they hide low in the view?

I hear discussion of my life like a rhino in a zoo,

The sheer conduction of this knife isn't high though when they do,

So near assumption in the strife that its side road is a U,

No one made the cob a pipe though if it christens in the cress,

So, I pray to God as mindful and I piss in my distress,

Past this prison in my death and my lawless, godly capers!

As it drips into their desks and it causes soggy papers,

Fish for flaws in funny waders since the pen is all black,

If the bras are money makers Mr. M has sold back,

Miss a bomb before the mist if an autumn mourns a fish or the sauce is as ashy,

It's a non-conformist kiss like the common corner kids with a toss of their candy,

Go and fade the shaded dot in the same reaction tree,

So, I'm made to break the knot like I'm Maniac Magee,

Pour a drink for the bands that are called on like they're debts,

'Fore I swing from their branch and I fall from there in death,

View the mound past the well if the sound isn't felt and it notes a distant day,

To the ground as I fell like the town into hell and the roads to disarray,

Though fine to most like tips so gray, it's an awkward gossip bowl,

So, I'm supposed to piss away but this knotted obstacle.

One Man's Refuge

Dusty pen for pun and arguments to learn depression is in threes,

Huxley's men were done with documents and turned attention to the trees,

They hurt me and my freedom as my hands would bleed in place,

They assured me I would see him with a chance to plead my case,

No one helps me in the office -

It's in interests of the guards,

Though they held me as a hostage,

With the whispers of the sharks,

The science doesn't get you if you profit from it lately,

Compliance is an issue in the closet that they drag me,

Gas will burn a leaf of late when it's dragged like it's me,

As they turn to leave in fate and I beg for a key,

A martyr made of ribs burned anointment in the former,

The guard that gave me cigs turned and pointed to the corner,

"Count your crows and hog tusks with your cocks cut to quick,

Now I know it's not much but we boxed up some shit."

In the damn bush's leshy is the hate of a god,

Then the ambushers left me to my fate like a dog,

Being tested for the tombs in towns that tether down hurdles,

Breathing heavy from my wounds and found a leather-bound journal.

The Scribbles of a Madman

Grind the grain out on farms from the plagues of thine love,

Time to lay down our arms when our legs are tied up,

Hips that hide guns and metal if their hate hums for Himmler,

With the prize comes a medal; with the race comes a winner,

Know we fizzle out in misery if many are the ministry,

So, we scribble out a syzygy and simply it's a symphony,

Set your compass in the bogs with a villain by the end,

Yeah, they hunt us like we're dogs, but we'll kill 'em like we're men,

Hook around and slap their optics looking east and so vain,

Put 'em down and grab the chalk stick; cook the beef like lo mein,

But alas, I'm alone and I'll die like an ant,

That is latched to a stone and then fried like a plant,

Cut the glass and the bone with the pie in the camp,

Such a task in its own and a sleight of the hand,

Half the rooms are spinning silly, I shall comment it as slowly,

As these fumes begin to kill me, I will document it closely,

Pin this circle to the ground in a mural of the mound if the evil eyelids touched,

In this journal I have found is a pearl that is bound to the people I have loved,

Should I spell nothing great if the book is found and I'm dead?

But I smell something faint and I look around to find it.

The Last Fisherman

Cast a window down the door as I'm wiping down a napkin,

As I scribble out my story and I write about what happened,

With this A-hole paid a buck for his carpool and his view,

It's a ladle laid in luck and the marble of the hue,

Tied if 9/10ths are late if the sign said it's 8 for the stupid cunts and crowds,

Like it's rye bread to bake and if I'm dead awake, then we do it once for self,

Passing moments like they're moons by the serum in a pack,

As I'm zoning from the fumes, I then hear them in the back,

Mirrors crumbling is a bad thing and it's harder in your pain,

There they're chuckling and they're laughing as they barter for my brain,

Fucks are found beneath the street if they're spirited and something,

Pushed around a piece of meat and I hear what they're discussing,

They walk around their evenings and they stand to feed their fame,

They talk about their seasonings and plan to eat my brain,

Hunt with whiffs - don't snatch the steak if you wouldn't look to steal,

But these pricks won't catch a break and they couldn't cook to kill,

Dawn my body like the wild when I sold my home for wings,

Mama taught me as a child when to hold my own with kings,

I hear the quakes and win so that the peaks are close to dust,

My tear escapes the window and he leaps for both of us.

Die by the Gun

Yo, we live by the gun and we die by the blast,

So, we sit by the sun and we fry from its gas,

Though we give like a lung and we cry like a mass,

With a tongue ring now to kiss more on ellipsis of the blade,

It's the one thing I'll wish for like the dishes that I've made,

If I come clean, I'll live more than the kisses of a date,

Miss the time that we give 'em in accosting at the car,

Risk the dime that we live on and the crossing that we mar,

Knowing fifths are five for winners and they try to still begin,

So, we live our lives as sinners and we die as filthy men,

Put this dowel to their vents if it's wrong as the reasons,

But the smell that I sense is as strong as the seasons,

Near a fall afternoon on the tarmacs of prison,

Here it's all caps like DOOM where their hardhats are given,

Dusty bread to pray for right when you knew to smoke the purp,

Huxley's men are day and night in their mood and mode of work,

Should I bind the bench's boards and fit in the newest restroom?

But I find the stench's source and it's in a bluish mushroom,

Here my trouble comes and comes and it never dies in fields,

There's a couple fuzzy ones and I recognize their gills.

Computer vs. Conscience

It rains up in this prison as it's grainy and it's colder,

I came to my decision and with Flamey on my shoulder,

How I'm living as a prophet is a kernel of the fact,

Now I'm sitting in this closet with this journal in my lap,

Diamond locks pinch the bougie as they spear fifty boys,

I'm at odds since they moved me and I hear Squishy's voice,

Come with me to seat the row with a quarter for deposit,

Suddenly I see a glow in the corner of the closet,

When it rained, I sought the sun and then rented the whole club,

When he came, he brought me gum and rekindled an old love,

The grave will never see us if we can't survive the hunt,

The taste remembered sweetness as it tantalized the tongue,

Take me back to pop a soldier on the road to bomb the draw bridge,

Flamey sat atop a shoulder and he spoke with common knowledge,

Fifty coins to bring us Godspeed like the pals that sell cocaine,

Squishy's voice was ringing softly like the bells of Hell's domain,

Count your ghosts up like they're beers as you're reaching distant kings,

Now they're both up in my ears and they're preaching different things,

Anybody dreading doubt as pity haunts a creepy peer,

Flamey wants to get me out and Squishy wants to keep me here.

PART IX –

"Grand Ball"

Yum! Bok Choy

Time to divvy eight cups if a heaven hears the cry,

I'm the limpy-legged fuck that they left in here to die,

By the sky's bleeding gums are the loneliest of prophets,

Why can I see the sun when they hold me in this closet?

Miss my kettle and my pies since my pies appeal to kings,

It's a devil in disguise as he tries to steal my wings,

Quaked and cracked as we're weathered; laid in lace and undertone,

Make him flap for his effort; make him raise a sun his own,

I suspect something is up, see and I fished a foot of villain,

I regret coming with Huxley and I wish I would've killed him,

My best limelight has a switch as I passed it to my mom,

I guess hindsight is that bitch that I asked unto the prom,

On the bed when in old wood and the benefit of cedar,

Mama said she was no good, but I never did believe her,

I set the world's old bombs to blow while burning with my crappy plan,

I met the girl so long ago while turning to a candy man,

Farm a separate bid of cider in the hallways fraught with girth,

Mama never did she like her, but I always saw her worth,

When we're ready for the win and the rich have gone to sleep,

Then she left me for the wind with a kiss upon my cheek.

Dust Amongst the Detriment

I've come to bury woe this year like any puppy's nose is clean,

I wonder where we go from here when everybody knows their scene,

There's no one team to go hunting and defend any fucking lie,

It's so serene to show something to upend when we up and die,

What is something I should comp if it's stuff I couldn't gift?

But it's nothing I could want when it's what I wouldn't give,

Cut the gubmint to its sticks like the right had did us dirty,

Put the putt into the bricks when I try to hit a birdie,

Much is solemn as the sound like a hell and hence its men,

But I've fallen to the ground and I smell that stench again,

Since it truly stopped my breath mints with choices due in pain,

It's a woolly blob of death since it poisons through the brain,

Picked upon a seedy vine set in crumbling-pie pity,

If they wanna eat me, fine, let them fucking die with me,

I show the sun no soylent like a hundred coins to wow,

I know this fun goes poised in what the fungus poisoned now,

Though I'm nothing but a pipe dream in the spiral glass cracked,

So, I'm pumping up my psyche for my final last act,

I'm dying like the soldiers that'll thunder here and leash us,

I'm crying on the solstice, but I wonder where my Eve is.

Imbibe for Epic Climbs

Knowing age in its numbers, though they camp us in their shoals!

Throwing sage to the embers so it dances on the coals,

Spite the fools that spar, box, or are cool with tossed discs,

Like a school of hard rocks for a pool of soft fish,

Stories sate the cup that's dry with mine filling by the beauty,

Lordy bake me up a pie when I'm feeling kinda loopy,

I'm inside of your mind with supplies and my guns,

I imbibe on the wine and survive on the crumbs,

Time to die for the crime and arrive on the fronts,

Hide the wife on a dime with her eyes on the cunts,

Punters running in to field 3 as they pass the cup and free doubt,

But they're coming in to kill me and I have a fucking freak-out,

I show God through the land when my burden is the sun,

I know not who I am, or the person I've become,

Clear the line and gunboat maybe if they soldier by the limit,

Here my mind is jumbled daily and it's over by the minute,

Why put this petal on me if the real skies die while drying?

I rub my temple softly and I realize I am dying,

Going 'wow' when there's enough room in the grimy dens of shit,

Owe a bow unto the mushroom as my mind begins to split.

Rising Sun Ruins

Dear Condolence, I ain't giving you the natures of my dojos,

Here for moments, I am flipping through the pages of my photos,

Dying in a cruel abyss that the degradations petrified,

Lying in a pool of piss like dementia patients left to die,

Come and cover high-wind noons by the pier with grizzlies feeding,

From the other silent rooms, I can hear of Squishy beeping,

Drown the rain and call it weak when it's raining on the grass,

Now my pain has all but peaked and I'm banking on the pass,

Wander off with this and blame me for the soldier that would say no,

Come to consciousness with Flamey on my shoulder like an angel,

Shroud the fury showing magic and to all orgasmic palms,

Now they're fiercely going at it with their algorithmic alms,

If the troubled quarrel runs live, then the song says that it sells,

It's a double-barrel punchline's with entendres as the shells,

Just a distant drop of dandy as the fire singed the ice,

But I miss my shop and candy with retirement obliged,

Bury oceans of the violence in the fane or wall to end,

Sharing moments of this silence with the flame I call a friend,

Might appear as a prophet, which we passed far and fed,

I could hear from the closet, Squishy asks, "Are you dead?".

An Ornate Agent of Chaos

Weigh a golden hue and goose as the cut blooms fade a speck,

Swaying salt unto the wounds as the mushrooms take effect,

Cut the costumes nape to neck when you run in for the fun,

But the hushed rooms sate the sect when to come in with a gun,

What's a one and plus a one with a hundred ones obliged?

Such to summon us a sun in the sundered sum of vice,

Since the hunters come at night, it's a one-up of the price,

It's another summer's rise in the come-up of the ice,

This an end fit for souls while you pump it in a pontoon,

Mr. M split the poles as he hunted with a harpoon,

Pinch your bible and your reins from the span and spire to the candy paint,

His arrival in the flames like the Man on Fire from *The Phantom Pain*,

Pay the loss what it earns, made from blossoming turns,

Make you watch while it burns, saved from gods and the ferns!

Is the pen weighed in feather or the country we add up with?

Mr. M made a vendetta, for in Huxley he had trusted,

Shall we bust in to the dungeon when the process is as moot?

Now we mustered what he just did with injustice in a suit,

List the ten words I spoke as you lick the glass candy,

Mr. M smirked and smoked as he flicked his ash at me.

Nana's Remedios

Strip the mattress with a spin in the conscience of a crime,

With the gnashes in my skin and the monsters on my mind,

As the bombed skies run in to the hogtied woman with her goals and her grief,

It's a long night coming with the wrong guy summoned in the coals of the quays,

Tasks and deeds are fast to die near the bomb I've set to bring,

As I bleed my last goodbye, there's a song I've yet to sing,

Go and pick the gun on up that the simple think fell,

So, I prick my thumb for blood in a thimble inkwell,

Paid to be the plant in place and shrug or shrink the wrong truth,

Made to reexamine greats and tug the strings like Don Bluth,

Sunken springs where logs ooze with a catfish-dry sardine,

Hunt the kings with dogs loose while their captives die starving,

Why depend on plight and destinies for the drinks of drama toddy?

I begin to write of recipes and the things my Nana taught me,

Swimming shifts in synonyms, and the dreams I book a cruise,

Spinning sticks of cinnamon in the streams of sugar cubes,

Stand in steam and brooks in boots with a handy blade and whim,

And it seems we look to lose with the candy made to win,

Show me back to break the bends with their ten tacky gods,

So, we had to make amends with the friends that we've lost.

Cleanout of the Century

This tomb is fed its tyrants as we stand tall but lower,

The room was dead in silence and the grand ball was over,

Clutching grams like lines of crack with a sober jaw and prenup,

Huxley's hands behind his back as he oversaw the cleanup,

The evil that survived was entrenched in fuckery,

The people that had died were as dressed in luxury,

Plus, we build in doubt that's passed to a hundred bill pulled,

Huxley wheeled them out and laughed with his stomach still full,

Shift the sand if it's a play in the grace of ball and stone

Mr. Madness on his way to the place he called a home,

Shroud the hall with purely clovers and the peach that luck poised,

Now the ball was nearly over like the feast for fuckboys,

It's assurance of the facts when they sell the sense of profits,

With the servants in their masks like the skeletons in closets,

Hatching plans least for days as the shotties hunt poker,

As the hands reach for plates past the bodies slumped over,

Piss that vision on the cones when they saw me on the spire,

It's baptism of the bones in the ennui of the fire,

Fly steps are spreading paper just to pluck the brow and eyelids,

My breaths are getting labored and I struggle now to write this.

In an Old Wooden Schoolhouse

I teach love is a weapon to attack the cycle next,

I reach up into Heaven and I grab my final breath,

Kiss the sky by sand and shell and the raspy rows ablaze,

If I die, I am in Hell and my candy goes to waste,

Know I'll guide 'em to the bend like the fish faced with caves,

So, I'll fight it 'til the end with my fists raised like flags,

Wanna lock me up a devil with a noose in heights strung,

Nana bought me but a kettle that I used when I's young,

There is fire as the wood graces a string on the wall,

To retire in a good place is a dream when you're small,

Here and dead to us are no direct wishes,

Sure to shed the dust that's so surreptitious,

Strike a match with a flail like it's math that you fail in an old form of reap,

Write the last of my tale by the mast and the sail as I go home to sleep,

Five for double cash and craze with the subtle cracks appraised,

Store a crate of sweets instead,

Ride the couple's path ablaze like a bubble bath awaits,

For the fate my Eve has met,

I must miss the good one pictured with the lanterns of the lair,

I just wish I could come kiss her from my caverns of despair.

End of the Denigrated Path

I fixed a fact so fleeting that a man then sheathes his quiver,

My lips are cracked and bleeding like a canyon cedes a river,

Buried planes that sold the setup like the saucy pots of grub,

Barely strength to hold my head up and I'm coughing blots of blood,

Come to inch in and sear money with the price to pay our plaything,

From a distance I hear Huxley and his knives when they are scraping,

Tasks are ticking tocks to tweak like the tusk tempers in tune,

As I'm drifting off to sleep, and then Hux enters the room,

Recursively a city as its death evolves for some,

He looks at me with pity and he says, "You almost won.",

Put the belt to watch us thrash like a ship as several sink her,

Couldn't help but cough a laugh as I flipped my middle finger,

"Come to cut up your man more for the sick streets to fit,

Motherfuck what you stand for; you're a rich piece of shit!"

Twenty miles in a cinch when ascension is ungrounded,

Huxley smiled like the Grinch as his henchmen then surrounded,

I was carried in a white sack on a crag with leap eternal,

I was barely fit to fight back as I begged to keep this journal,

Pussy blood from the bed hides in hell to reap the wraith,

Huxley shrugged as he said, "Might as well keep the faith.".

Baptism in Blue Fire

It's raining on the climbing wall and happy if it's something fair,

They dragged me to this dining hall and strapped me to this fucking chair,

I'm past defeat and candy once the argument is subtle,

I asked to keep my hands free just to document my struggle,

Shifting sands and signs they stack must be good to wash me, brother!

With his hands behind his back, Huxley stood and watched me suffer,

Tears are bagging up the weed leaf in the zeal of zany sands,

Here I begged if I could see Eve with the feel of Flamey's hands,

I'm supplied with the flecks and imbibe on the flesh as I bring along the peas,

They denied my requests with their pride in my death as I sing a song of seas,

Such is happiness in hurdles to believe I like it gory,

But they granted me this journal with reprieve to write my story,

Half the cabinets are now free as they read the buckle's gold,

As the ravenous surround me and they keep their knuckles cold,

Busing miles to the last leaf par per many past perps,

Huxley smiles and he asks me, "Are there any last words?"

Find us smoking in the soot plumes, each the same old broken sky,

I'm just hoping that the mushrooms eat my brain so then they die,

Though I'm broken and I'm lifeless, I'm alive and need a friend,

So, I'm hoping as I write this, I survive to see the -

PART X –
"Fin"

Outro [Skit]

The large stone that Sal and San were sitting upon was located directly outside of the dining area of the downtrodden manor, and though old and aging, the massive bay windows surrounding the outcropped room let Father and Son see the grisly scene frozen in time within. . .

Sal and San pushed their helmets to the glass window doomed to eternally crack as they glanced through and saw several skeletons in black robes seated around an oval table close to the back of the room.

A lone skeleton sat slumped over in a rickety wooden chair in the middle of the room with its skull cap removed and sitting on the floor next to it.

San thought for a moment before asking his father, "Daddy, do you think that one by himself is Gaspar?".

Sal nodded solemnly as his son piped up with one more inquisitive question for his dear dad, "How do you think his journal got out here then?".

Sal thought for a moment before replying to his son, "Kid, I think it was scavengers most likely."

It didn't make any sense. Sal had read the entirety of Gaspar's story to his son and in doing so still had not discerned several key points he had failed to decipher.

The exposed sun was rapidly setting over the mountains in the drawn-out distance, and Sal put his arm around his son's shoulder as he said to him, "I love you kid. I don't know why bad things happen to good people, but I do know that you should never ever quit trying to be a good one. Look what happened to this good world when bad men were allowed to destroy it."

Father and Son began their trek back to their airship as San started to skim through the pages of Gaspar's journal and when he got to the very last poetic entry, he realized there was one more page stuck to the back of it.

San nearly stopped in his tracks as he read two last words, *"Love Eve"*.

www.ingramcontent.com/pod-product-compliance
Lightning Source LLC
Chambersburg PA
CBHW050833180626
46814CB00004B/1594